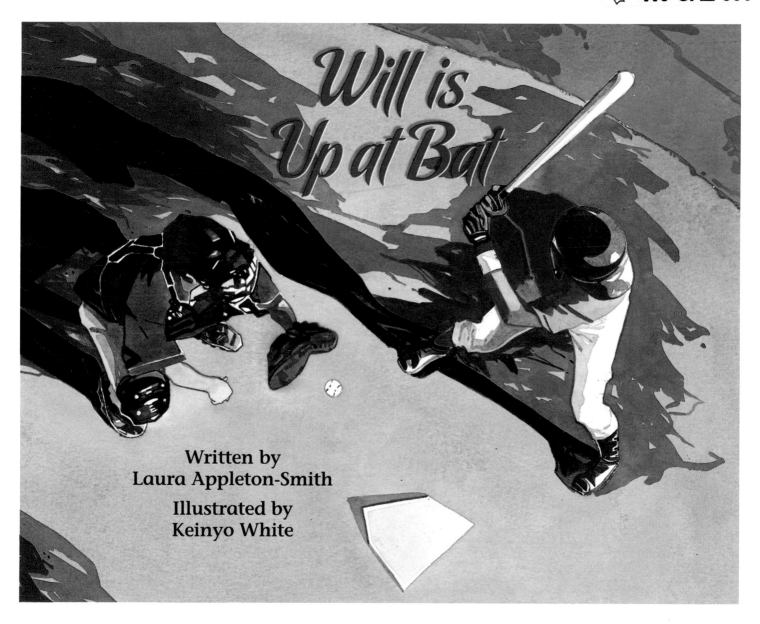

Will is Up at Bat

Written by
Laura Appleton-Smith

Illustrated by
Keinyo White

Laura Appleton-Smith holds a degree in English from Middlebury College.
Laura is a primary school teacher who has combined her talents in creative writing with
her experience in early childhood education to create *Books to Remember*.
She lives in New Hampshire with her husband, Terry.

Keinyo White is a graduate of the Rhode Island School of Design with a B.F.A. in illustration.
He currently produces children's books and freelance illustrations
from his studio in Los Angeles.

A Book to Remember™
Published by Flyleaf Publishing

For orders or information, contact us at **(800) 449-7006**.
Please visit our website at **www.flyleafpublishing.com**

Eighth Edition 2/20
Library of Congress Catalog Card Number: 2008937539
Soft cover ISBN-13: 978-1-60541-008-1
Printed and bound in the USA
243081021A10

For Willem.
LAS

—

For Ajani and Scarlett.
KW

"Tap, tap, tap." Will is up at bat.
Will taps home base with his bat.

Will lifts the bat and fixes his grip.
The pitcher pitches his pitch.

Swing and…miss.

"Strike 1!" yells the ump.

"Tap, tap," goes Will's bat.

Will lifts his bat and fixes his grip.
The pitcher pitches a second pitch.

"Let that pitch pass," Will tells himself. "That is a ball." And it is. "Ball!" is the ump's call.

"1 ball, 1 strike," the ump tells the fans.

Will's mom and dad yell, "Go, Will!" from the stands.

The pitcher pitches a fast pitch.
Will swings and…it's a hit!

14

The ball is up and Will runs fast.

"Go, Will!"

First base is in the past.

The ball lands on the grass.
Will is still running fast.

18

The ball is in the second baseman's hand.

Will is getting to third base,

and he has to make a plan....

20

Will plans to run as fast as he can.

As Will drops in the dust and slips into home base,
the ump yells to the fans...
"Safe!"

24

Prerequisite Skills

Single consonants and short vowels
Final double consonants **ff**, **gg**, **ll**, **nn**, **ss**, **tt**, **zz**
Consonant /k/ **ck**
/ng/ **n[k]**
Consonant digraphs /ng/ **ng**, /th/ **th**, /hw/ **wh**
Schwa /ə/ **a**, **e**, **i**, **o**, **u**
Long /ē/ **ee**, **y**
r-Controlled /ûr/ **er**
/ô/ **al**, **all**
/ul/ **le**
/d/ or /t/ **–ed**

Target Letter-Sound Correspondence

Foundational Skills
Consolidation

Story Puzzle Words

base	pitches
baseman's	safe
pitch	strike
pitcher	third

High-Frequency Puzzle Words

first	home
from	into
go	make
goes	to
he	

Decodable Words

1	drops	himself	miss	second	the
a	dust	his	mom	slips	ump
and	fans	hit	on	stands	ump's
as	fast	in	pass	still	up
at	fixes	is	past	swing	Will
ball	getting	it	plan	swings	Will's
bat	grass	it's	plans	tap	with
call	grip	lands	run	taps	yell
can	hand	let	running	tells	yells
dad	has	lifts	runs	that	